For June, with love

MAX AND THE LOST NOTE copyright © Frances Lincoln Limited 2009
Text, illustrations and design copyright © Graham Marsh 2009
The right of Graham Marsh to be identified as the author/illustrator of this
work has been asserted by him in accordance with the Copyright, Designs and
Patents Act, 1988 (United Kingdom).

First published in Great Britain in 2009 and the USA in 2010 by
Frances Lincoln Children's Books, 4 Torriano Mews,
Torriano Avenue, London NW5 2RZ
www.franceslincoln.com

Acknowledgements

A tip of the beret to: Ben Shahn, David Stone Martin and Terry Southern.

Also the following cats must get theirs: John Gall, Joakim Olsson, Glyn Callingham,
Sam the Cat, June Marsh, Jack Cunningham, Max and Coco Katz, Tony Nourmand,
The Crew from the Island, Nicole and Tony Crawley, Janetta Otter-Barry,
Judith Escreet, Yvonne Whiteman, David Cutts and Richard Riddick.

British Library Cataloguing in Publication Data
available on request

ISBN: 978-1-84507-972-7

Illustrated using a dip pen with nickel finish Leonardt nib. Black outline
in Rowney 'Kandahar' Indian ink coloured with Dr Martin's watercolour inks
on Saunders watercolour paper.

Set in Bulletin Typewriter

Printed in China
9 8 7 6 5 4 3 2 1

MAX AND THE LOST NOTE

WRITTEN AND ILLUSTRATED BY

GRAHAM MARSH

F

FRANCES LINCOLN
CHILDREN'S BOOKS

This is Max. He's a cat who plays piano.
Max is a sharp dresser – some cats say he is
as dapper as Dan and hip as Harry. That means
he is a very cool cat indeed.

One day Max was writing a new tune. Music filled the room and notes were falling from the piano like snowflakes – when suddenly he stopped... Max had lost one of his notes, and could not finish the tune.

Max looked everywhere for his lost note.
He looked right, he looked up, he looked left.
He scanned the whole room for the lost note.
He even looked in the suitcase which he kept
neatly packed in his room.
"I know," thought Max, "I'll see if any of the
other cats have found my lost note."

So Max rode his scooter downtown...
stopping at Kitty's Place for a
glass of milk and some catnip.
At Kitty's he met The Felines.
The Felines were a famous vocal group.
There were Florence, Phoebe, Ella and Coco.
They wore groovy clothes and were
always singing.

KITTY'S PLACE

MAX

Max asked The Felines to sing for him – perhaps his lost note was hidden in one of their songs. No luck. The note was not there. Then Coco said, "Try Long Tall Dexter. He has plenty of notes."

Max told Long Tall Dexter about his lost note.
"Well, let me see," whispered Dexter. "I'll play something for you
on my saxophone and we'll see if it's there."

When he had finished playing, Max said, "That's a solid tune, Dexter, but my lost note isn't there."

"Now listen, Max, my furry little friend," said Dexter. "I know three cats called Miles, Oliver and Charlie who might just know the whereabouts of your lost note. Tell them Long Tall Dexter sent you."

As it was such a warm sunny day, Max left his scooter and red jacket at Dexter's house and decided to walk.

Max met up with Dexter's cats. There was Miles who played trumpet, Oliver who was a drummer and Charlie who played a mean guitar.

They played some funky music for Max... but sadly, his lost note was not there.

Max was beginning to think he would never find his lost note. Then he saw his neighbour Rita sitting on a bench playing her flute. "What's happened, Max?" she asked. "I've lost a note," replied Max. "Is it this one?" Rita asked, and she played a beautiful melody on her flute. "I wish it was," said Max. "That was sweet."

Suddenly Rita had a thought. "Go and see my friend Sam," she said. "He has a new double bass. It is so big, your missing note might just have landed there."

Now Sam, like Max, was a very cool cat indeed. He had a different hat for every day of the week. That's a total of seven.

The mellow notes coming from Sam's double bass made Max feel very relaxed. Max said, "I like your music very much, Sam – but my lost note isn't there."

Max walked home. On the way he listened to the sounds of the city: the birds, the cars, the buses, even the fat cat selling newspapers. There was a kind of music in everything, if you took time out to listen. Max heard all the different notes the city had to offer - all except the one he had lost.

When Max got home, he sat down and kicked off his shoes.
Suddenly he saw something that made him nearly jump out of his seat.
There, stuck to the sole of one shoe, was his lost note! He must have
trodden on it while he was writing his new tune.
"So," thought Max, "the note wasn't lost after all – it was just missing!"

Now Max could finish his tune.
All the cats joined in, and
they sang and played for hours.

Max was one happy cool cat.